More Praise for How to Sit

"By turns powerful, playful, innovative, and always blazing with a kind of hard truth, this collection is full of music and magic and messages for the reader and the world. I loved this book so much."
—Amber Sparks,
author of *The Unfinished World*

"*How to Sit* by Tyrese Coleman is a memoir of uncommon candor and emotional resonance. Reading this collection, I hardly moved, hardly even breathed. Such is the power of the truths spoken here in Coleman's precise and beautiful, startling prose. A must read."
—Kathy Fish,
co-author of *RIFT*

"Tyrese Coleman offers stories and essays that are brilliant, vulnerable, hard at times, and unfailingly generous in their scope and honesty. Every piece has its own strength, its own life, its own importance—but what unites the work as a whole is Coleman's incredible gift for narrative and the faith her voice inspires, even when you aren't entirely certain where fact ends and fiction begins. I only wish this book were longer."
—Nicole Chung,
author of *All You Can Ever Know*

"*How to Sit* is, at root, a reflection on how to live. How to both accept and transcend your past. Coleman excavates her personal history, sometimes in stories handed down from past generations, sometimes in DNA results, and she discovers that it's the act of writing itself that can free her from her family, her guilt, maybe even herself."
—David Olimpio,
author of *This Is Not a Confession*

HOW TO SIT

HOW TO SIT

Tyrese Coleman

Mason Jar Press | Baltimore, MD

Cover design and layout by Ian Anderson

Published and distributed by
Mason Jar Press
Baltimore, MD 21218

Learn more about Mason Jar Press at masonjarpress.xyz.

To my family, especially my grandmother, whose smile I will always remember.

Exhaust the little moment.
Soon it dies.
And be it gash or gold it will not come
Again in this identical guise.

—Gwendolyn Brooks, *Annie Allen*

A Note from the Author

The process of remembering involves the storage of information and the subsequent retrieval of that information. Memory is not static. Memories are not facts. For many writers, their ability to recall certain events becomes the point of distinction between whether their work is nonfiction or fiction, i.e. true or made up.

How to Sit challenges the concept that a distinction needs to be made when the work is memory-based, because memories contain their own truth regardless of how they are documented. This collection, a memoir when viewed in its entirety, plays with the line between fiction and nonfiction as it explores adolescence, identity, grief, and the transition between girlhood and womanhood for a young black woman seeking to ground herself when all she wants is to pretend her world is fantasy.

This collection of nonfiction and not-quite-nonfiction is intended to make you wonder what is and what isn't true, and whether or not that matters. *How to Sit* asks you to examine how these perceived truths of fiction and nonfiction speak to one another within the same space, forcing you to pull up a chair and have a seat inside the space in-between.

STORIES/ESSAYS

How to Sit

Grandma slapped my foot, uncrossing my legs. *You think you grown? Sitting in <u>my</u> house, with your legs crossed like you a damn woman.* Her bleached nurse's uniform was starched, stiff as stale white bread, stuck to her syrup-colored body. She confronted me, hands on hips, waiting for a reason, waiting for me to open my mouth.

We argued—something to do with the phone, or something to do with a boy, or something to do with me walking around her house, around men, with no bra, or with my mother—who lived with her man, never with my grandmother, even as a child, even as a baby—coming by her house pregnant and tall and mean.

Or something to do with their fight—Grandma wanting to get my mother back by messing with me, I don't know. The fight where I watched my grandmother kick my mother's swollen belly. The fight where my mother, a seventy-pound and eight-inch advantage, pushed my grandmother, held her wrists above her head and yelled, *I'll put my finger in your face if I want.*

Or was the argument really about me? Grandma's forty-seven-year-old body still wore a size eight, but the small titties sagged. And she was short—much shorter than my thirteen-year-old frame, one with plump breasts a man fondled during one of her house parties—my fault, she said—and legs instigating anger, making her smack them open. Jealous.

She waited for a reason. Virginia Slim Ultra fierce against burgundy lips, they twisted at the only thing she had over me—I lived in *her* house. *Don't you forget it.* And, I was not going to sit in front of her with my legs crossed like a grown-ass woman either.

———

A picture of her dancing: legs cut from frame but hips jutting, arms outstretched, torso exposed, hair solid gold, sweater sucked on, hand clutching a drink and cigarette, red eyes slanted towards an afroed man. Grandma partied with Marvin Gaye in DC. Boogied at Studio 54 in NY. Stayed places her family had only seen on TV. She was wild.

She disappeared at sixteen after my mother was born. Grandma's older sister is who my mother calls "Mama." My grandmother returned to the country, to her home, just twice, to drop off two sons. She never did settle down, always on the move.

Diabetes brought her back for good.

When they took her leg, I didn't see the stump. Not naked anyway. I imagined it purply-green, swollen, pus-filled, and, thank God, she kept the little white stocking cap on the end as if it were the head of a newborn baby.

She wasn't crippled. She still partied. Sold shots of whiskey in the back room—"my" room—for fifty cents. The house full of smoke, I leaked water in my eyes from toilet paper I wet in the sink. In the living room, bodies gyrating, and Al Green singing he was so tired of being alone.

Still saw the married white man, too. The one who looked at me funny, like the men who touched me at her parties, legs crossed or not, my fault or not. When he came over, she made me leave. When he left, she suddenly had money for Captain D's.

But she never left the house. Not even to feel the outside. And where was she going anyway?

————

I am sitting on her nursing home bed. Grandma adjusts herself, raising the stump as if she intends to cross her thighs. Instead, she lowers it, stretching her full leg out. Her toenails are close to my leg. They are daggers. And if they were attached to her fingers, and if she were forty-seven and not sixty-seven, she would use them to scratch my face for pitying her.

Thirty minutes away from here, down I-95, past the truck stop, left on the dirt road, about a mile in, you will see a "For Sale" sign and the neighbor's goats eating her neglected grass. She wants to go home, she says, more than once. But, Medicare will only allow her the one they pay for. No assets.

My mother braids my grandmother's hair. It is a limp, flat sheet. The stump is stripped bare. It moves side to side as if groping for something lost. I lean back, ankle resting on the opposite knee. It is only us women, but Grandma says she wishes I would learn how to close my legs.

Why I Let Him
Touch My Hair

I sat beside a white boy in a dead bar. Alone, he slurped beer, watched football. Hair yellow like an unpeeled onion, no signs of sun on his skin. A typical white boy. No match for me, yet, I started it, impressed him with what I knew white boys liked: Metallica, tits, *Seinfeld*. He was nice. Bored, I guess. We talked for a while. Both in our twenties, both southerners. I desired his attention because he didn't give it freely. He spoke anxiously. An awkward laugh followed every statement, every eyeball-dash at my cleavage, each concerned glance upward at the wild black kinks springing from my head, and then, each nervous scan behind him, around the room. His fear empowered me.

In fifth grade, I fought a white boy beside a stack of gym mats. He touched me down there. I looked like a China doll, my aunt said, fingering my jet hair. Sizzled-straight, it framed slender shoulders, stuck against my skin by hair grease and sweat. She favored me. They all favored me. Lighter than my cousins, my honey complexion drew their wrath. *White Girl. Think you cute.* Headaches from pulled hair. Arm scratches from fighting. I fought him, at least tried. We never played together. He chased me around the gym, cornered his prey. We were children, just children, and maybe to him, that was what children did. But there was authority to his touch, an exerted right, his God-given right to me. Because I was pretty. He said I was pretty. For a black girl.

Another laugh, another glance around. My new friend took in my hair again, so I asked him what he thought about it. He said it was cool. I scooted closer to him, my cleavage slow dancing in his eyes—up, down, out, in—with every breath. I offered: do you want to touch it? We had an audience, another black woman beside me. I ignored her. Her disapproving stare should've told me something, the way she shook her head to herself. I offered him: do you want to touch it?

A white man used to visit my grandmother. He was married with kids my age. He drove a red truck, flying down our dirt road like it was his. I'd get home from school or playing and see his truck in the yard. The rule: *don't go in that house when that truck in the yard.* Middle of the day, face red with sweat—I remember him flushed and always smiling—brown mullet glued against his neck. He'd walk right on in the house, no knocking or nothing, as if it were his. I grew up in front of him. By thirteen, he looked at me funny, but most grown men did. Now, he'd come, and I'd leave, or I'd stay, and he'd give my grandma the money right in front of me.

Wenches: what we were called during slavery.

And without me seeing it, I knew he did that every time—every time, he gave my grandma money like she was his.

———

In college, I let the white boys I worked with see my tits.

We were friends. The bar was slow. I wasn't the only girl flashing my breasts that day. It was alright.

My title: *the* black girl. The only one, surrounded by white boys. The conversation: the color of my nipples. Were they coffee-colored with large areolas? Were they saggy *National Geographic* tits? I laughed. We were friends.

It was alright because of that time that drunk guy called me a nigger, and they threw him out. Cool because they liked rap, were from Baltimore or Philly, their boy was black.

White boys who talked about the Asian hostess' sushi.

White boys who said they'd never date a black girl, even if she was pretty for one, or friends first.

White boys who wanted to party with my black girlfriends after work—three, four in the morning. And when I said no, they're sleeping, white boys who demanded I wake their nigger-asses up.

White boys who refused to apologize. But we were friends, though.

———

Now, at a different bar, a different white boy extended a shaky hand toward me. I lowered my head. Who knows what I expected being petted would feel like. His touch was surprisingly soft. He rubbed my hair, only bending the ends.

Done, he cried, "I did it!" His accomplished smile. My power disappeared. If it had ever existed to begin with.

Prom Night

Outside fogging car windows, empty parking lot lights glowed like part of a fairy world T wasn't allowed in. X, still wearing his tux, passed the blunt toward the front seat to his boy dressed in a white tee; he hadn't gone to prom. The radio played 90s hip-hop—money, cash, hos, moneycashhos—they rapped along. The fairies outside her window were blond and pristine with stars for eyes and gold-coin titties. Could heavy-breasted black girls be fairies? Nah— her magic was lost at ten when her mother's boyfriend fingered her, taken when men at her grandmother's parties grabbed her, made her sit on their hard laps and bounced, bounced, bounced her soft baby-girl body against dirty construction clothes rotten from sour Wild Irish Rose. Gave the magic away at fourteen to an older boy who said he loved her. What else was she supposed to do with it? So, did it matter if she let these boys have some of it, too? Did it matter if they laid her flat, pressed her face against the blue leatherette seat, did a Chinese fire drill around the car to switch places when the first was done, high-fiving on the way around like teammates through an obstacle course, while T suffocated silently until every drop of any magic she'd ever had was gone?

She sucked the fat brown tube when the blunt came her way. Her fingertips tingled unpleasantly. She shivered in the boiling car. X said her hands were cold. He kissed her. It was wet and messy despite his soup coolers. His breath tasted of stale cigars and McDonald's chicken nuggets. T and X were alphas: smart, popular, college bound. His friend, she couldn't remember his name, was the Nobody, the Dope Boy, the Sidekick. Nobody was the poor kid the hot guy friended in elementary school, or his cousin he shared sloppy seconds with.

Nobody faced the steering wheel while T and X kissed. She sensed Nobody's hard-on, lingering in the air with the weed smoke. What did he think, that this is how it happens in pornos, his anticipation a tight spring before release? She knew nothing about him, and his power scared her. X pulled away. Nobody faced T. She stared at her shoes.

Nobody got out of the car—was it too late to say no? X massaged up her thigh. She looked over the front seat through the windshield to a haze of black, golden darkness, like Christmas, wishing she could fade into the land of the little white fairies, fly into the iris of a glowing dot of light between dark trees with notched, shadowy holes. Be magical, like what she'd dreamed this night would be.

The headlights of a security service car turned a corner, tiger eyes burning brightly. Nobody jumped into the front seat, turned the engine over, and drove off. The boys wanted to park somewhere else, roll a new blunt, drink more beer, listen to more music, and run a train on her.

But—the engine's vibration. The car's motion. The taste of open air, fresh air—warm, spring air struggling to breathe while summer sits on its face—the taste, the caress over her bare shoulders and open toes. A spell broke. She made them stop the car. Eyelids half-shut, she walked home in her slinky dress, her pumps glittering an unearthed enchantment across the blacktop.

I Am Karintha

"Her skin is like dusk on the eastern horizon,"

When I read *Karintha*[1], I think about Preacher. His hands were thick and covered in white ash like chalk over black pavement. He would grab my wrists and as I twisted my arm around to get away, the inside of his hand ground into my small arm. I was around five with hair down my back that my aunt said made me look like a China doll. Preacher smelled like dirt and whiskey and he was so black he scared me. He always wanted me in his lap, hobbyhorse, the point of his dusty pants jutting from in between my knuckle-like knees.

When I read *Karintha,* I think about my mother's boyfriend. My mama said he got money, and we stayed with him at his trailer where I had my own room with a bed I was too afraid to sleep in. I was five. I sung "you know I'm bad," slapped the rhythm of the Michael Jackson song on his gut, hugged him. At night, I snuck in between them to sleep. And, in the night, with my mama on the other side, his fingers went in between.

---

[1] *Karintha* is a short story found in Jean Toomer's novel, *Cane.*

"O can't you see it, O can't you see it"

When I read *Karintha,* I think of my cousin's daddy. I was thirteen, I know for sure. He was drunk—just like everyone else in the house. So drunk, how could he remember what he did? And I was lying anyway. He smiled a whole lot. People liked him. He came in my room that night and touched my big breast. He told me not to tell. I did. Grandma said I thought I was grown.

When I read *Karintha,* I think about D. The preacher's son. He was a senior and had a car. He took my virginity on his bedroom floor when I was fourteen. I cried and asked him to take me home. He bought me jewelry and said he loved me. He had big teeth and a thin, bony face. I told him he made me sick. Jamaal punched him out in the cafeteria at lunch, and his feet flew up over his head. I broke up with him and did it with Jamaal who made me cry on the bathroom floor 'cause I loved him so much.

"Her skin is like dusk on the eastern horizon"

When I read Karintha, I think about Leland, Poodie, Tanky, Nema, Masud, Jide, the Police Officer, that divorced guy, Pat, Kenan, Kegan, Kyle, Kwame, Kenyon, my old boss Chad, Chad's roommate, I think about telling that one guy his thing was too small after he bought me a pair of Timbs, I begged him not to leave, I made Harry come get his shit, I think about cheating on Neil in the Bahamas, I think about that guy in Miami and walking through the streets of South Beach, too drunk to know if I had said yes when I really meant no.

"…When the sun goes down"

Sacrifice

My mother throws a manila envelope through the car window, gets in slamming the damn door, making my old-baby—Bullet is what I call her, my old-baby Silver Bullet—rattle like the bag of bones she is. I want to peel out of here now, make a mark, tattoo treads over the Spotsylvania County Correctional Facility parking lot. But, I'd probably have to pay for that, too.

"Where you going?" I say.

"I got to get something from Ronny's, then take me down Aunt Liza's." My mother rifles through the envelope with her name, Shelby Walker, on the front. She throws her worldly possessions on the dash one by one: Chocolate Kiss Victoria's Secret lip-gloss, a pair of hoop earrings, a dead iPhone encased in pink fur—

"T, you got a charger?"

"I got Samsung. It won't fit."

… a pack of Kool Milds, the "O"s resembling handcuffs, a cigarette lighter in the shape of a fist flipping a middle finger—she uses the last two, blowing smoke out the window that comes right back in.

"Ma, Ronny has a restraining order against you."

"I need to get my shit." The word "shit" sounds like "thit" with the cigarette between her teeth.

"Ma—"

"What did I say?" Locked up for three days, she looks sleepy and wild, a feral cat hungover. She hasn't washed her face. Black mascara bleeds around her eyes as if *she* were the one beat. Chipped, dirt-lined nails clench her cigarette, the lit end circling near my bare shoulder—the shaking tip slowing, with each suck and blow.

This is a bad idea. But, whatever, if she wants to go back to jail, that's on her. If she wants to keep fucking up, lose her job over some stinking-ass man just because he has a house and pays her cell phone bill, that's on her. Didn't anyone teach her she could buy her own house? Well, no. I guess no one would've.

Ok, here's the plan: pull up LA-gangsta-drive-by-slow down the dirt road leading to the house, turn off the radio when we get to the graveyard, park on the other side of the trailer, next to the barn, make sure she doesn't slam the goddamn door again, pray he isn't at home, you, as in me, sit in the car, preferably smoking one of them Kools as you try to stay cool, then peel out of there when she runs back to the car, house probably up in blaze behind her, hair blowing in the wind with her "fuck 'em girl" strut, flicking a cigarette back into the flames like Angela Bassett in *Waiting to Exhale*.

"Ma, you remember *Waiting to Exhale*?" I lean into the seat's embrace. Might as well get comfortable.

"Yeah."

"Whitney Houston was good in the movie."

"She was alright." A bare foot, big toe fancy with airbrush, is folded under her, tapping to Beyoncé on the radio. "Angela Bassett made that movie." She turns up the radio and stares out the window. I see the mood is not a talking one.

The window is down, and wind whips my face. The air in my ears is softer than this silence. My arm is out, palm flat, working hard to stay stiff so it doesn't bend from what's trying to push it around. I miss country roads, only a ditch with a torrent full of trees on one side and a solid line on the other to stop you from running into oblivion. I miss lying in the grass behind Aunt Liza's and seeing the sky leak gold through swaying branches. Trees are interesting—despite their bending; you never see them break. Not unless they're struck by lightning or someone cuts them down. Outside forces, right? I miss feeling unbreakable.

The middle of the day, twelve-oh-nine, and I just busted my mama out of jail. Aunt Liza always said that's where she'd end up. She's lucky this is her first time.

I inhale deep and let out all the air inside me in one long whoop. The cry is louder than the wind. Much louder than those howling voices that told me I should let her ass rot. Wilder than the thoughts claiming she deserved it, even when I reached Aunt Liza and she begged me, pleaded with me, then rebuked me saying God would punish me if I didn't use everything I had to get my mother out. And it took everything I had. All twenty-five hundred of it. All twenty-five hundred dollars and eight months working in the English Department for full-time hours and part-time pay. All twenty-five hundred and six months taking double shifts, waitressing in the AM, bartending in the PM, every Saturday and Sunday fighting drunk, sweaty palms off my tits. Twenty-five hundred dollars—storage fees, yes, and tuition for one more class—everything I had, since she never taught me how to hold on to a dollar, or a man, or a job, or a college career. This sigh, my suffocated roar, would be alarming to most. Hell, it scares me.

My mother acts as if she doesn't hear a thing.

"Ma, you know I came down here for something else."

"Aunt Liza told you I was in jail and needed to get out. I know."

"You don't remember the storage auction?"

The radio DJ smears vinyl, winding one song into the next. And she still has nothing to say.

"Ma, I don't have money like this."

"I'll pay you back. That's why we going to Ronny's."

"What are you going to do if he's there?"

"Don't worry about it, it'll be alright."

"Oh, my God! How are you going to say, 'don't worry about it'?" She raises her thin, overgrown eyebrows at me. I taper the hysteria by gripping the steering wheel tight, twisting my palms around as if it were her neck. Her cigarette is on the edge of newly shined chocolate-glossed lips. A hint of sweetness puffs the wind, blowing hair wild over my forehead. Her mouth is tight around the speckled end so she can't talk, changing the subject.

I sigh again, less ferocious.

"What happened?"

She offers the open end of her soft-pack. I take a cigarette. I need a cigarette.

"We got into it. He told me to leave. I wasn't going nowhere. So, he called the police. Domestic assault or some shit."

My mother will be thirty-eight this year. October.

Her tank-top says, "Don't you wish your girlfriend was hot like me," sans question mark.

My friends, my college friends, my Georgetown, black-student-union friends trying to prove they are down, even though they went to private schools and drive BMWs like everyone else not cashing in on affirmative action and financial aid as I am…

well, was, I guess

—those friends and I laugh at women who look like my mother: fake hair, fake nails, and fake eyelashes—"food-stamp fancy." Us, the Afro-Punk intellectual bourgeoisie, with our naturals from the Black Power Movement, our Back to Africa, A Tribe Called Quest circa 1990 Kente cloth jeans, and our Talented Tenth loafers—The New Black Aesthetic—we've stolen our ancestors' creativity with no real sense of what we're doing with it other than wearing it on our bodies and pretending we know where it all comes from and what it all means. My friends and I, we laugh at women like my mother who have the misfortune of wearing ill-fitting factory made-in-

Meh-he-co clothes and processed hair, because…oh, God bless her, she don't know no better.

But, I've digressed.

She handed me a beer at my eighteenth birthday party. I tried to give it back, wrist limp with the weight of it. What kind of ghetto-trash mother encourages her under-aged daughter to drink? What kind of mother at all? I wondered if any of my friends, my high school friends, saw her. Though if my high school friends—girls just as poor as me, taking care of younger siblings or their own kids, with ombre burgundy-tipped weaves and eyelashes grazing their foreheads, girls who knew I was different, knew come five, ten, fifteen years from now, I would be doing anything but being like our mothers (FUCK! I let them down)—if *they* had seen her give me the beer, they would've thought nothing of it.

Shelby Walker said I was "too cute" to drink with *her*. She knew I'd be around the corner, sitting on the hood of some boy's car, smoking weed or drinking or fucking, so if I wanted her to ignore that, if I didn't want her to "punish" me, then I needed to sit down, cross my legs, and have a goddamn beer with my mama. She laughed and pushed the can at me again, a few cold drops shocked the web between my thumb and forefinger. I laughed, too, although what she said wasn't funny, true as it may have been.

My mother's ass crack smirks at me over her jeans. Her head is between her knees. The rest of the envelope contents are on the floor: A small change purse and a few dollar bills.

She grunts, "You need gas money? I got seventeen dollars. There might be a Walmart gift card in here somewhere. You can buy something for your new place."

The radio mixes another long zip of pulled wax.

"Have you bought an outfit for graduation?" She says sitting up, wiggling herself straight. "Everyone has taken off work. You said anyone can come right? We don't need tickets?"

I wipe sweaty palms over my thighs, turn up the radio, and shout, "Don't change the subject, Ma."

She lowers the volume. "I just want to make sure everything is straight." She claps and says, "Okay," getting down to business. I don't know what has bought on this sudden energy, but I don't want it, don't like it.

"So Aunt Liza is coming, of course. She gone want to see her *baaayyybiiii* walk across that stage." I hear her smiling. I can't look at her. "You should think about getting her something. Her birthday is that week. Be nice for you to show your appreciation."

"I know."

"Nettie can't make it. Her part-time won't let her take off. Kurt said he'd rent the van."

Please, stop talking.

She's so thrilled.

She's smiling. Smiling so wide the sun is picking up the silver in the back of her mouth, glinting dots, like bullets, across the dash.

And now she's chatting, chat, chat, chatting. Chatting so much all I can make out is the smacking of her lips, the flapping motion of her slick lips, smacking and flapping and chat, chat, chatting. It's making my stomach hurt.

"Ma, how could you do it?"

"Huh?"

I pull the car over so she's slanted sideways in the ditch. Even with my face in my hands, I see her looking down at me, suffering me. "Why are you so damn dramatic? You're like some fucking white lady," she says.

No tears, though they're stinging the edges of my eyes. "You let all my stuff go to auction, Ma. Everything I own. My TV, my journals, my clothes. I have nothing. You know why I came here."

"That shit's more important than your mother?"

"No, but you said you'd pay it. You said 'don't worry about it.' They kick me out of school, housing, food, everything, in a week."

"I didn't have the money." She blows smoke. Gray hovers in front of the open window, a blemish against the yellow-green perfection of the woods beyond it. "That was *your* bill," she says.

"If you didn't have the money, why didn't you tell me? Why would you even offer?" She doesn't respond. She never responds. "I should've known I'd be paying for it anyway—like the car insurance and everything else you said 'don't worry' about. When do you ever do anything right? All my money went to get *you* out of jail."

A MoneyGram commercial mocks us.

"Come on." She brushes the air with the back of her hand and looks out the window, "I don't have all day for this foolishness."

"It's all gone now, anyway," I say, turning the engine over. "The auction was at twelve." With a little extra gas, I straighten out and get back on the road.

We ride in a welcomed yet hardened silence I want to bang my head against until it's a bloody mess.

Daddy said the fighting is why he had to let her go. I can't imagine them together in the first place, let alone tolerating one another long enough to make me. Friends talk about how their parents' divorce fucked them up. Shit, I'm glad my parents were never married. What would that even look like? My father coming home every single day to the both of us, one an ex-convict man-beater, the other a college kick-out, instead of his bougie six-figured wife and her manga-porn-addicted freak of a son?

Probably to do with my grandma and how my grandpa used to beat her…maybe how Grandpa started a new family and Grandma ran off and left Ma to be raised by Aunt Liza…that's why my mother likes to fight her men. Or, she doesn't trust herself to be happy. Or fighting is her way of exerting control and independence. Relying on someone else for everything—a place to live, a ride, a fucking life—she controls nothing but her men. Fighting makes her feel like a person.

Her boyfriend before Ronny, Marco D. Snopes, aka Swagger D, the top of his head thick with waves, looking at them too long would make you seasick, the type of guy who showered twice a day with Cool Water body gel, wore a silk wave cap at all times, even while he worked, even when at the store, unless he was going somewhere special: the mall, out to eat, church. They met at the carry-out. Swag had no chance. Shelby Walker is blessed with a body meant for catching cases. My mother's ass moving inside skinny jeans is like two country hams fighting for space.

They were good together. Swag liked to drink. Not a drunk; it wasn't like he needed a beer first thing in the morning, just pissy every evening after work. He'd come home falling down, they'd fight, my mother yelling he needed to be better around me; this wasn't the example she wanted me to have. Example of what? A man? A relationship? A mother?

One night, the middle of the night, he burst open my bedroom door. His shape stumbled in and out a tube of light from the streetlamp outside the apartment window. His hand cupped his cock like a toddler holding in his pee. I laid still, not the first time one of her men came for me, as if they assumed we were a buy-one-get-one-free deal. Swag didn't seem like the molesting type. I guess none of them did. But, there had been so many, first impressions didn't mean shit. None of them had the balls to get their dicks wet. Instead one fingered me when I was five, another had a thing for putting me on his lap and bouncing me up and down, his arms around my stomach, his forearms right underneath my breasts as they bumped his bare skin, dick solid against my prepubescent sacrum.

But Swag just thought my bedroom was the bathroom and pissed in my laundry basket. Second time I saw Ma give a grown man a black eye over a load of dirty clothes—more money at the laundromat. Now that's something to fight about.

He drove us to Georgetown when I moved on campus. We were lost, kept going in and out of Virginia, mainly because my mother couldn't believe we were in the right area. She screamed at Swagger to check his GPS, this couldn't be it; this couldn't be where T's going to *school.*

Mercedes, Bentleys, Land Rovers lined the outside of my dorm. We parked Swagger's old Expedition with the rusted bumper in the loading area behind the building, next to the dumpsters.

We hauled cardboard boxes and black trash bags full of my life into the cinder block cube that was my new home. That moment culminated years of hustling, of convincing people I was smart and deserving, that I was "a role model for younger kids, fighting against the odds," as the old white lady presenting my UpWard and Mobile Scholarship said. A full-ride. Five interviews, three sweat-stained suits, and hours of massaging my jaw muscles loose before they finally said I won. But, it's easy being the best student in a shitty school, and liberal white people trying to make up for the fact their ancestors owned my ancestors love to give charity cases like me cash to assuage their guilt. Mama always said never turn down a free meal.

I looked forward to those meals. I looked forward to a bed that was going to be all mine for four whole years, one that wasn't rotating, and didn't move towns, counties, apartment complexes, trailers, every couple of years or months, every time she broke up with one man and found another. A bed I didn't have to share with my mama and her fingering boyfriend. A bed at Aunt Liza's when there wasn't another for me anywhere else.

My mother didn't speak. She and Swag unloaded in silence, comparing my trash bags to my roommate's Louis Vuitton luggage. She gave a limp hand to my roommate's mother, a blonde, white woman wearing sunglasses on top of her head, two superimposed "G"s for Gucci winking on the sides. She didn't want to meet the resident assistant. She wasn't concerned about partying and drinking, and what were the rules again about boys being in the dorms after hours? She didn't want to help me decorate or go to the dining hall and have one last good look at me. She quit early and left alone.

Swag and I found her later by the truck. Shelby had bummed two cigarettes from the janitor, the only other black man in all of DC, it seemed. She lit her Newport, closed her eyes and exhaled her own suffocated roar. She pulled me into her. She was soft. Her hair was cold against my face. She smelled of nicotined cocoa butter and oniony underarms. She held me tight, I tried to pull away, but she squeezed her arms around me, holding me until I relaxed and laid my head on her shoulder. I even closed my eyes.

She whispered, "Don't believe you belong here," then let me go.

Right now, she's directing me by putting her hand in my face. "Ok, make a left right here."

"Ma…"

"I don't want to hear all this nonsense about that damn auction." She's yelling, "I am the worst mother. You've made your point. But, shit, you haven't even asked me how I'm doing?" She's hysterical, "I just got out of *jail*. Do you care about that at all? Shit's always about you?" She's facing the door jamb. I can't see her face. Maybe she's crying. I doubt it.

I should just tell her I'm not graduating. She can't be mad, I just bailed her out of jail.

What did they expect? They sent me to Georgetown. What the hell was I doing there? There is an art to bull-shitting, *she* taught me that. I crushed Chaucer, slayed fucking African Cultural Modernity, butchered Elements of Political Theory, but ask me—for real—ask me for the concrete: Numbers, figures, real dollars and sense. There's no bullshitting when it comes to Calculus. You either got the answer or you don't. I never had the answer. The letter came too late to do anything about it, my last semester and all. And Ms. Coulter, that basic bitch from UpWard and Mobile, said the scholarship covered me eight semesters, not until completion.

Twenty-five hundred. All I have. One more class.

Yes, my mother is indeed crying.

The car is quiet again minus the music on the radio. I take her hand, lacing our fingers. Our palms are sweaty, our fingers are slim and long, my complexion runs into her complexion. We ride that way, regardless of how awkward it is to steer, until we reach the entrance of Ronny's dirt road.

And I creep LA-gangsta-drive-by-slow.

The song on the radio reminds me of how pretty my mother is. It is, "If This World Were Mine," and against my thoughtful plan, I let this song play at a volume others can hear. Alone, I sing the female duet using my cell phone like a hair brush or curling iron, eyes closed, of course.

My mother slow-danced to this song at a cousin's wedding. She was a bridesmaid and wore a gold, silky dress matching the color of her skin and hair, "Honey Blonde" according to the box. She danced with some man who tried to grab her ass. She moved his hand, squeezing it so hard he shook his fingers out when she let it go. Her eyes were closed, red lips moving to the lyrics as if they were part of that slow-dance along with her legs, her hips, her shoulders. She'd taken her shoes off because the Payless, twelve-dollar, gold-glittered heels had broken the skin on the back of her ankles and she couldn't walk in them anymore. Her toenails were unpainted, raw and infantile. Even in bare feet, she stood up straight, back arched perfectly with a grace only a dancer or a truly beautiful woman has. Somewhere in the history of past lives, my mother was Cleopatra. I don't have that. I will always have to pull my height up from the bottom, heels, calves, thighs, taut so people can see me standing in a crowd.

She finished dancing and sat down, pulling me into her by my waist. I smoothed back her hair from her face. I said I wanted to be her. I had to be eight or nine, no older than ten at the most. I know this because it was before I got angry. I wasn't tired of her immaturity yet; I wasn't ashamed of her yet, and I had not yet figured out my mother was a real person and not my best friend. My mother hugged me, and said she wanted me to be everything she wasn't.

<hr />

There she is, running to the car. I turn the ignition. This is it. I'm here for you, Angela. Let's burn this bitch.

She's waving her arms above her head like she's trying to hail a taxi or a runaway bus. She's breathless, grinning like a damn fool.

She opens the passenger door, grabs her manila envelope and starts re-packing her worldly possessions one by one.

"What are you doing?"

"Ronny's here. He ain't mad. I'm staying home."

She runs to my side and pokes her head into the window. She kisses me on the cheek and draws out a roll of cash from her pocket.

"I was saving this for you. You can use it for the storage. I didn't know all that junk meant so much to you." She can't help but roll her eyes. She takes my hand and presses the cash into it, "there is a little more in there, too. I think about six hundred. Should be enough. Something nice for graduation."

"Thanks." I squeeze the cash until sweat molds the paper. I don't even mention the bail money, her fine from the county, the cost equaled everything I had. I don't want her to know she was right. I don't want her to know I didn't belong there.

I pull away using too much gas, my tires eat gravel rocks and the rear slips. The radio is playing some rap song with a repetitive sing-song chorus that repeats over and over again in incessant, idiotic loops.

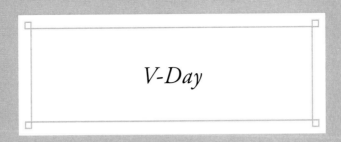

V-Day

"V-Day"—on the pregnancy blogs, message boards, and websites—means the day you reach 24 weeks. My V-Day, my viability day, was on February 14, 2013.

Viable. Oh, what a magic word. "Able to live at birth."

This is how I celebrated V-Day: I took a selfie in the dining room and posted it on Facebook, officially announcing my pregnancy to the world. I drank two glasses of red wine with my friend from law school. Later, when I went to bed, I watched a porno with Vanessa Del Rio in a three-way and masturbated until I passed out.

I hadn't had sex for 140 days. 20 weeks. Almost five months.

For me, being pregnant was like that R. Kelly song from the 90s: my mind was telling me "no," but my body, my body was telling me "yes." Almost every night, my unconscious relieved the latent sexual stress gathered inside me, and while I slept, my uterus thumped to climax. The OB, always the conservative one, told me to stop it. The specialist said it didn't matter and congratulated me, it seemed, on my telekinetic power of vaginal manipulation. Regardless, on V-Day, I was relieved. I thought I didn't have to wait anymore.

I was 24 weeks pregnant. Less than twenty-four hours later, I went into labor.

————

When I went into labor that first time, the doctors kept saying I should wait four more weeks before going into labor again. As if I had anything to do with it.

They wheeled me to the ultrasound room and positioned my chair outside in the hallway to wait for my test. There was a train of wheelchairs lined up, each occupied by a tired-looking woman. We didn't speak to one another; there was no need. The woman directly across from me rolled her thumbs around one another as she waited. Her long fingernails looked like the fake ones from a child's Halloween witch costume, and I wondered how long she had been on the inside. What did she do to get locked up? Her shoulders were thin, the hospital gown like paper, never relaxing over her bony frame. I thought about speaking, but I didn't. I didn't want to make friends. I didn't need to make friends. I wasn't going to see this woman again. I was going to make it to 28 weeks. I was going to go home, lie in bed, and reach 32 weeks. I was going to go back to work, dressed in all of the cute, expensive maternity clothes

I hadn't worn yet, and when I got too big to walk around, I was going to take the agency's Rascal Scooter back and forth down the halls, like the elderly people you see cruising down the sidewalks near nursing homes, until I reached 36 weeks. I was going to make it. I couldn't wait.

The ultrasound results: the blood flow had returned. I just knew it. I knew I had convinced the universe to love me. My hands were clean. My palms were hairless.

My cervix had begun to open on its own sometime near the end of my first trimester. My doctors placed me on bed rest. They also put me and my husband on medically-induced abstinence, since the stress to the uterus from an orgasm coupled with my incompetent cervix posed too much of a risk for pre-term labor. But things had already been dry; fears of hurting the wee ones flared up in our minds whenever we undressed, killing the mood.

So when the doctor said no sex, I rolled my eyes. Ppsshhh, what sex? I felt emphatically unsexy. My legs were so hairy, I could comb them with a brush. My underarms looked as if I had Chewbacca in a headlock. No matter how many showers I took, there was something about lying in bed all day that made me feel funky, and no, not in a James Brown kind of way.

I felt like I'd been in bed for an eternity only after a few days. I didn't understand how that rectangular piece of cushion I laid in, sweated in, and drooled on could ever lead to anything other than misery and boredom. I wanted out of the bed.

…I wanted into the shower…onto the floor…on top of the kitchen counter.

…I wanted Stringer Bell and Dr. Jackson Avery.

…I wanted Alex Pettyfer and Channing Tatum in slick rain jackets and G-strings Magic Mike-ing all over my bedroom floor.

Bed rest involved lots of television watching.

My cervix continued to open. At 22 weeks, the doctors—my multiples pregnancy being so complicated I had two doctors—suggested intervention. My OB prophesied this occurrence at our very first meeting, telling me that miscarriages in the second trimester occur when the birth canal opens up for no damn reason and the baby falls out. She said those words to me: "the baby falls out." The specialist performed a cerclage, stitching my cervix shut. I remembered the OB's words as they gave me my first ever epidural. I was awake, feeling only pressure and pulling as I watched a team of nonchalant physicians poke away inside my numb womb. I began to hyperventilate. They gave me something like Valium. And my boys continued to hold on.

I remained confident that the universe was on my side. My sons had already survived two surgeries; they wanted to be a part of this world. My cousin called to check on me after the cerclage. Her sister had a baby at 26 weeks, she said. She told me to take it easy. She knew what it was like, seen what could happen. Her nephew is autistic and doesn't speak much. I told her don't worry; I got this. I had a premonition they would come early. Most multiples do. They were due June 5, 2013, but I expected their birthday would be sometime in May. How beautiful—a spring birthday party in the park.

Pregnancy is waiting. It takes time to grow someone.

They admitted me to the hospital after the ultrasound, transferring me from one bed to another with the hopes that my stay would be temporary, just until I reached 28 weeks. I stocked up on DVDs—*The Lord of the Rings* trilogy, the *X-Men* series, and others—and organized the unread books on my Kindle that were collecting dust on my virtual shelf. I was ready to serve my bed rest sentence armed with everything I needed to fight monotony. My dear, sweet husband sent me videos of him walking our dog, Luna, in Rock Creek Park. I watched *Harry Potter* DVDs and listened to Stevie Wonder on my phone at night while I tried, in vain, to rest.

I couldn't sleep. No, it wasn't more nighttime uterus knocking keeping me awake. My nerves, maybe even my maternal instincts, put the smack down on my prefrontal cortex's smut slinging. No more nocturnal emissions for me.

I couldn't sleep because my doctor's orders were that I stayed under observation. Nurses were continuously in and out of my room, messing with me, sticking me with needles and catheters, giving me pills to swallow, and screwing with the heart-rate monitor. My stomach, slippery and sticky from ultrasound gel, was belted with a Doppler machine that had to stay on. One of the babies had diminished blood flow from his placenta. That little tube his cells threw together wasn't very efficient.

They prepared us. The specialist asked if we wanted to risk a premature birth of our healthy baby to save the life of the other one.

Did I *want* to? What kind of question was that?

————

After 25 weeks and five days, the C-section took no time.

My boys came out breathing.

They rolled me into the NICU after sewing me back together. I laid back on a gurney, another bed, my stomach empty. The lights above me ran down the ceiling as the nurses made lefts and rights to take me to my sons. I remember seeing a transparent box, bright tanning lights, hearing lots of beeps, different kinds of beeps, noticing flashing numbers, so many tubes, and two tiny babies the size of rutabagas wearing sunglasses. I cried and told them to take me out of there. Guilt was pressing a bony kneecap on my sternum. I couldn't breathe.

———————

81 days. 11 weeks and four days. Approximately three months. That's how long we waited.

The NICU is full of people waiting.

There are babies waiting to feed, waiting for surgery, waiting for oxygen, waiting for medication, waiting to see their parents, waiting to be held; some wait to be loved. There was a teenage couple in our area of the NICU whose baby was three pounds of chocolate sweetness. When the nurses dressed her in pink, she looked like a Hostess Snowball. The couple was hardly ever there to see her. I overheard one nurse say the little girl was going to think *she* was her mama. There were a few evenings when we would see them there, slouching in plastic chairs, never touching, never speaking to the child. I wanted to steal that baby, take her to a friend, someone I knew whose maternal clock had run out of batteries, but could still feel the hands of time moving inside of her. The hospital staff called the kids more than once with the happy news—come pick up your baby, she's ready to go home. The parents didn't show up right away. When they did, they packed their baby's luggage, her heart rate and oxygen monitors, and disappeared.

In the NICU, there are parents waiting to take their babies home. Some just wait hours. Some wait days, weeks, months. Many wait forever. I worked while the boys were in the hospital, choosing to use my medical leave for when they came home. But there were days where I would take off and spend hours there, sitting in the terrible wooden rocker between their Isolettes, staring at them as I desperately milked my breasts with a machine like an industrial farm cow, willing myself to produce something natural while surrounded by all the artificial. I left NICU room "B" and took a lunch I bought with me down to the hospital lobby to eat. I happened to meet that woman from the wheelchair train, the one with the long fingernails. She had had twins too—a boy and a girl. She delivered at 28 weeks, a goal I once had for myself. Her daughter died in utero, also suffering from placental insufficiency. We exchanged email addresses. She never wrote me back.

Doctors and nurses wait; their anticipation measured in the dipping numbers of a heart rate, the increasing hum of a ventilator, or the progressive beating of a pulse-oxygen machine. Langston, Baby B, was small. The diminished blood flow had stopped his growth. He was one pound, three ounces at birth, the average size of a 23-weeker, the size of a baby one week too early to be deemed that magical word. Yet, Langston was the calm one. He was small, but he had hardly any problems. He breathed well. He gained weight. He learned to suck and swallow. He was our Mr. Incredible.

But James. James, my Baby A, was probably the most like me. In his hard-headedness, he took on every stereotypical preemie complication with the rebellion of a teenager. He was the average-sized one, weighing one pound thirteen ounces at birth, normal for a 25-weeker. He should have been the easier patient, but as the nurses and doctors used to say, "You can't trust a preemie."

James had heart surgery. A titanium clip smaller than the size of a pencil eraser was permanently placed inside his chest to close one of his blood vessels. James had eye surgery. A man wearing glasses used a laser to blast abnormal cells from inside my baby's eyes so that he didn't suffer from the same disease that blinded Stevie Wonder. But worse than all of that, James had an infection. The doctors again prepared us, showing us x-ray images of his chest, his lungs resembling a tree covered by clouds of locusts. James had necrotizing enterocolitis, a disease that is one of the leading causes of death among babies in the NICU. If they don't die, they receive surgery. Their intestines are removed, feeding tubes are inserted into and attached onto their bellies, and they face a lifetime of long-term disabilities.

That was my baby's possible future—all, I thought, because I couldn't wait to cum.

After praying one night in the hospital's chapel, my husband and I went home. I lay in my bed, the scene of the original crime, still smelling the acetone scent of antiseptic foam coating my hands. I always cleaned my hands before I touched them. Because I was unclean. I couldn't wash away my guilt. Because there is no worse punishment for sin than guilt. Guilt crushes you, paralyzes you and makes you see who you really are. Even when James recovered with medication alone, I didn't take that to mean that God had answered my prayers, or that he forgave me as I had before. The guilt held me back from being happy. It replaced my confidence with fear.

Now, my restless nights were spent facing the white tube of light from my cell phone, looking into the future. My internet searches: "cerebral palsy and premature babies," "25-weeker, autism," "developmental delays." I had imagined, as some expecting parents do, my boys' future. My husband and I talked about teaching them to ice skate at two, how cute they would be pushing the little blue buckets across the ice with puffy gloved hands and red cold-pinched cheeks. We talked about how they would be handsome and popular. I imagined hating anyone who would try to date my sons yet feeling overwhelmed with joy and pride when they settle down and have children. We talked about their education and talents; it was inevitable that our sons would be intellectuals, brain surgeons, or musical virtuosos. We talked about sports, my husband forbidding football and me not keen on being an ice hockey mom, sitting on cold bleachers yelling at other five- or ten-year-old kids trying to bully my boys. But, I would do it. I would scream and shout and cheer on my talented, athletic, good-looking, successful, intelligent, able-bodied children with all the vigor of a woman ignorant in her privileged bliss. Now, I wondered if they would ever even walk. Would they ever even talk? Did *I* take away that future?

Guilt is a bully holding your arm as you try to run. Both of my sons got bigger, they both passed their car seat tests, they came home with oxygen but were tube-free in a mere two weeks, they gained even more weight at home removed from the stress and noise of the NICU, they thrived, are thriving, and yet...

One night after we had brought them home, I became hysterical. I held onto James; his cheek pressed against my chest, sweaty. My husband reached for him, and I felt like running. I was going to run the hell out of there with him. No one was going to take my baby. He was mine. He was alive. I had him. I cried and screamed, I don't even remember what for or why, but I was going to hurt my husband if he tried to take my baby. When I calmed down, my husband took him from me and told me to rest. I lay down in our bed, repulsed. I never wanted to touch myself again.

———

Whoever came up with the cliché, "time heals all wounds" is an asshole.

Time doesn't heal *all* wounds. It may dull the pain of some of them; help make the scabbing, the healing process, more tolerable. It may make you forget that you were even injured, for a moment, but time doesn't heal everything. Time—waiting, anticipating, wondering, hoping—can make things worse, and when those unhealed wounds inevitably reopen, you feel all the pain again.

As they reach almost 26 months, I have two healthy, active, and playful toddlers, but I am unable to rejoice in the small victories, always wondering when the next catastrophe is going to take place. Langston isn't talking. His vocabulary is limited to "da-da," "na-na." I find it hard to believe my husband when he tells me that the boy said, "hey" this morning, or that he pointed to the dog in a book, thinking it's my husband who just can't face reality. He doesn't know that God hasn't forgiven me. All I can do now is wait for it, for whatever is coming next, and in between, try to live. So, yes, even after having them, even after V-day, I am still waiting for viability—my own. Patience has never been my thing. I struggle with graciously accepting delays.

I Been Changed

Mighty Clouds of Joy played in my *Sesame Street* cassette player the old folks had stolen for their party. The room, tight with drink and singing, sucked light like my aunt's burgundy-painted lips wrapped around a Virginia Slim. I saw the room through a haze of gray cigarette smoke. A side table lamp lit the room in gold, romantic to my eight-year-old eyes. Uncle Pick and Cousin Baby Sis squared off in competing stances, arms and mouths wide, voices whiskey-warmed in the dark rectangle that was my aunt's living room turned sanctuary.

Pick sat. The rounded end of his stump poked out his shorts as it bobbed up and down—as if it still had a calf, as if it still had a foot, as if the heel of that foot stomped to the beat, as the other full leg remained unmoved, thinking it didn't need to work. Once, I sat on the floor next to that stump and took his glass full of liquid the color of Coke after ice melts, and downed it without asking. He watched me gag from the fire, cough orange-red flames from my chest. He scolded: *that's what your little ass get*, and I ran away before he could grab my arm and smack it.

The songs were not the hymns we sang at church, and I wondered had they made them up. These were lyrics about sinners, overcoming sin, holding to God's unchanging hand. They sang as drunks do, oblivious, full of misplaced heart, of unconstrained emotions that warped their faces in twists of pain or happiness—I couldn't tell what. *AhhIII know I been changed*—and Baby Sis took my face in her hand, her fingertips wet and cold as she smeared a thumb across my cheek. She was a vet, too, like Uncle Pick. Korean War for her, Vietnam for him. Now they both drank Strong Brown, sang too loud, argued about who had it harder. Pick saying Baby Sis, being a woman, didn't know what she was talking about and needed to sit her ass down. And Baby Sis—she won't afraid to knock a cripple out.

Pick moved me onto his lap. I watched his hands. His fingers, swole, fat all the way down like burnt-brown hotdogs, flickered as if playing piano in the air. *Whomp whomp whomp* went his hollow claps, and I thought maybe his palms couldn't uncurl, so used to having a Flintstones glass or cleaned-out jelly jar topped full of Strong Brown inside them. They didn't know how to flatten to smack and make sounds anymore. This is why I was never afraid of him, no matter how much he screamed in his sleep, or fussed when I dropped things and made loud noises, or when, after taking what he said was medicine, his eyes were glassy, wet balls searching for something on the walls only he could see.

Baby Sis did the stomping for them. Her short, curly afro seemed glistened, appearing wet and in a midst of smoke. She stood in the middle of the living room, shaking the slat floors and vibrating the small house—about ready to bring down the curio so that my aunt had to say *calm down, Bay, calm down now.*

She sang for Fergie, her best friend, who she'd met in Korea. Fergie, round and brown, as my uncles said, was the only one who could calm Baby Sis when she was drunk and looking for a fight. When she cried her mama didn't love her no more. When she feared going to hell and told my Grandma not to change clothes in front of her because God hadn't healed her sickness yet. Then one day, Fergie didn't come around anymore.

Tears filled the valleys of Baby Sis' face. She begged God to relieve her, to take the feelings away. She knelt before me, took my arm, pressed her eyes into the soft flesh inside my forearm. Uncle Pick jerked me back: *don't you touch her.*

My aunt pried me from their hands. I bit the inside of my cheek, tasted blood, but the tang could've just been in the smoke, in the memories they fought for absolution, memories that dripped from those songs with hanging melodies like cliffs we should all jump from. I know now why they both wanted to hold me. My small body was an altar to offer worship, to fill up with their sin or at least bear witness to it, so that in some way, I could take it away. Sometime later, when I hold my children tight to my breast, my skin hot from drinking all day, I'll wish I could pour my sins into them, and know I, too, have been changed.

Thoughts on My Ancestry.com DNA Results

REGION APPROXIMATE AMOUNT

I. Africa, 69%

A. There were chains. History books always describe the chains. Thick, heavy chains the width of a baby's forearm. This baby is carried close, so close to mama's breast. Mama wants to press, press, press baby through her chest so baby crawls back inside and down into her womb and never sees the light of this day. This day they march paths clinking with linked chains across a continent in the sun, the rain, the cold. The cold is no longer felt on their skin; it is just more weight on their bodies. So heavy, they pray the weight will bury them in the land. So they can grow into trees, *white* bodies walk around—seven, eight, nine times—with snapping branches that strangle white necks like chains the width of the Forgetfulness Tree. These chains, always the chains, the width of fists, the width of wide mouths screaming or wailing or closed in fear or beat shut or silenced with cut-out tongues, the width of leather-braided snakes slithering, biting across legs, slice naked backs on the way to Ouidah. But this baby, this mother, these soon-to-be slaves, are not my ancestors. I don't know who they are.

B. But I envisioned a man. My paternal grandfather. I met him once. His dark brown skin was the same shade as my father's, blacker around the eyes and lips. A slim man, the same height as my dad, he had our family's signature nose. That man resembled my dad so much that I think even the lines around their mouths—nervous smiles, easy frowns— were the same. The meeting was brief. My father and I had ridden to Richmond to see my grandfather at his mother's house—my great grandmother's house—one day when I was in high school…or maybe middle school…the time we spent so short and inconsequential, I can hardly remember when it was. My father didn't tell me where we were going. We just appeared at a row house in the city. He introduced me to a woman, a mean-looking black[1] woman who resembled a man, sitting on the couch in the living room. I realized at some point after we left that I'd just met my grandfather and great grandmother for the first time—the only time.

---

[1] Not "black" as in the ethnicity, but "black" as in her skin, the color of darkness.

William Zinsser wrote in his essay "How to Write a Memoir," "One of the saddest sentences I know is 'I wish I had asked my mother about that.' Or my father. Or my grandmother. Or my grandfather." I didn't say anything to my grandfather other than "hi" and "bye." When you are a teenager, so *affected* by boredom, it's impossible to care about anything other than the lyrics to your favorite song, or the name of the boy you like, or the lyrics to his favorite song. My father now mentions his father to me in passing every few years: "Had to go see about *him*," he says. "Oh yeah?" I say.

I began an online family tree a few months ago. I was afraid to call and ask my dad for his father's name[2] and date of birth. I sent him a text. I entered my grandfather's information, hoping to receive little, leafy "Coleman Family Tree" hints that would help me find out more about him. As Zinsser further explains, "Only when they have children of their own—and feel the first twinges of their own advancing age— do they suddenly want to know more about their family

---

[2] I didn't even know his name. I wasn't afraid that my father wouldn't tell me his father's name, but that he would ask me why I didn't know, and I would have to explain to him and say, "It's because you and my mother were never married. It's because I only saw you on the weekends and holidays as a kid and it wasn't until I was practically an adult that we became close." Or I'd say, "You told me he abused your mother, and that she had to divorce him because she thought he would kill her." Either way, how the hell would I know his name?

heritage and all its accretions of anecdote and lore." This is true. That teenager meeting her paternal lineage for the first time wasn't listening, was not interested, and couldn't care less about the man and woman sitting with her in that room, let alone their *heritage*. Ancestry is a comfort used to ease the passing of time: if we tell the tale of those before us, then those after us will tell ours. And during the storytelling, we will live again. But, that is the concern of the dying, and I, at that age, was immortal.

I no longer will live forever, and I owe my two black sons something more than just their great-grandfather's name. The melanin from those trace African genes manifested differently in my son, James. We called him James Brown the first year of his life. He is darker than the rest of us. One day when he isn't insulated inside the family bubble, he will understand the luxury of his brother's, his mother's, his father's light skin and feel the lack of it sting his own. I already see it happening: The doctor taking blood is gentler with my fairer son, apologetic— doting even—but he pricks James over and over, angry he cannot find a vein while James' screams wail through the office. The white parents on the playground who prefer to ask questions about his brother, "Oh, what's *his* name?" never to inquire about James, they just aren't interested in him. This is why we stopped calling him James Brown. It was a stupid joke anyway. Maybe he will pretend to be adopted when he gets older, pretend not to belong to us. I will understand. I know that I owe a due diligence to learn why generations of my father's fathers' faces are etched over his.

C. Benin/Togo: 33%. What I know is that my paternal ancestor lost. He lost the battle against King Agaja, because if my ancestor had won, he would not be my ancestor. If he had won, if he were a king or a chief, he would not have been sold by his king or chief. If my ancestor had won, artists would've made carvings of his face out of wood and brass. They would pay tribute to his sons in Lagos. Those sons would ride around in fancy cars wearing fancy clothes and fancy jewelry with fancy wives. I'd be Yoruba or maybe even Igbo. Ancestry.com says we share DNA, but that is why this is called an "ethnicity estimate" and not a "cultural match finder."

If my ancestor had won the battle, they would not have gathered up all his kin. They would not have tricked his son into walking near the shore to see the amazing boats, then tied him up and starved him so that later he would die and be thrown overboard. And those witnessing would not have wished their souls were in his body instead of the bones, the weight, they carried.

My ancestor would have been locked inside an iron face mask that only allowed him to see straight ahead. And, not far. Not *this* far, where his future and my past meet, and I know his name. He could only see the second ahead of the second he lived because the second after that he may have died—and he would not have been my ancestor then, either. Saw only straight ahead because, really, what was there behind him? What he was leaving—a name, a country, a family, a legacy—he wasn't coming back to, because he is my ancestor, *and I am a black American.*

He lost. Or maybe he was so strong, so virile, so much a warrior that he threatened King Agaja, the great King of Dahomey, and was sold out of jealousy. Or maybe he was kidnapped and forced to lie in a dark hole next to the woman with the baby girl who isn't my ancestor.[3] Either way, he was destined to lose. Dahomey fell. Colonialism won.

D. Or, maybe it is 1619 and British pirates have commandeered the boat my ancestor is chained to. It is night and a man who reminds me of Captain Hook[4] threatens to slice the throats of the Portuguese seamen operating a ship containing Angolan human cargo sailing for Never-Never Land. Said cargo eventually arrives on the shores of Jamestown, Virginia, 67.6 miles away from my hometown.[5]

---

[3] But, maybe she is yours.

[4] Because my sons are obsessed with the Disney Channel show where children outsmart a sea captain dressed as a British nobleman disguised as a French slave trader.

[5] The town of Ashland, Virginia, the so-called "Center of the Universe,"

The scenic Alt 95 route from Maryland to Williamsburg, Virginia, is dotted with historical markers and tourist traps commemorating the colony. My husband and I once drove the rural route for my cousin's wedding on the campus of William and Mary. She married a white man in Wren Chapel, which was built in 1695, when Jamestown was still the capital of the colony and Williamsburg was called Middle Plantation.[6] Our ancestor, the one on that boat, laid the first bricks for that church. She could have. She could've been a laundress who washed the clothes of the white men studying there, touching her there. She could have scrubbed the floors and cooked the food for those men who dragged her behind the building she built, tore her dress away, stuck themselves inside her, and made more ancestors that would eventually study at that college and marry a white man inside the building she built.

When John Rolfe described the meager purchase price paid for our ancestor who laid that first brick—that very first American slave trade—maybe he didn't consider the fact that his wife, Pocahontas, could've been sold for that same thrifty

---

located in Hanover County, once home of the largest slave population in the entire State of Virginia, the same state where slaves were first brought to America, the real center of the universe.

[6] I find power in this act, a great "fuck you," to the years of oppression, segregation, and dehumanization approved of within the walls of that place.

deal, too. Or maybe he did know that, and Pocahontas was already laying down bricks at another historic site, washing clothes for other historical men, and being brutalized while waiting for such honors as Disney to recreate her likeness and the State of Virginia to mark her footsteps along the alternative rural route to I-95.

Who knows?

II. Europe, 29%

A. Surname "Coleman" of Irish and English origin. According to Ancestry.com, "Anglicized form of Gaelic Ó Colmáin 'descendant of Colmán'…English: occupational name for a burner of charcoal or a gatherer of coal… English: occupational name for the servant of a man named Cole. Jewish…Americanized form of Kalman. Americanized form of German Kohlmann or Kuhlmann;"[7]

• Or, the surname of a plantation owner who made his slaves take his last name;

---

[7] Full disclosure, here is all my whiteness: Europe West (France, Germany, etc.) 10%, Ireland 9%, Trace Regions 10% (Scandinavia 4%, Great Britain 3%, Finland/Northwest Russia 2%, European Jewish 1%). Oh boy, I'm white, y'all.

- Or, because, later, when the first census takers after Emancipation came around asking for full names, my relative wasn't quick enough to say "Freeman."

B. One day when I was in middle school, my mother came to pick me up. I was outside, standing next to a white boy from my class. We both watched my mama as she approached. It was a beautiful day. My mom had long, straight black hair that the wind blew around her head with ease, as in a Pantene commercial. As she approached, the sun, shining on her from an angle, lightened her face. I laughed and said to the boy next to me, "My mama looks like a white lady." He stared at me confused, then back at her, a woman he had never seen before, a tall woman with pale skin and yellow undertones—"high yellow"—with long, straight hair, and said she *was* white. He said she wasn't my mama because that woman was white. And by omission, I was not.

My mother? A *white* woman!

My mom is one of the blackest people I know. Not "black" as in skin the color of darkness, but "black" as in a *Southern* black woman. My mother cooked pigs' feet, cleaned chitterlings, and fried a mean chicken leg. She was loud and said *chile*, and *mmm hmm*, and *nigga,* and laughed with her entire chest. She loved Gerald Levert and Luther Vandross and had a poster of Michael Jordan hanging on her wall, all her chocolate men. She made sure to tell me when I was not "black" enough: When I talked "proper" like a white girl, or listened to "white music"; and *ooo* the fit she had when I went to the movies with a blue-haired, grunge-dressing white boy…

She was angry. Friends and cousins pulled her hair, called her names—"white girl," "stuck-up." She built a rep around her temper. My mama would fight anyone, for any reason. She did not marvel in the luxury of her light skin. She battled to define her blackness by any means necessary. Because it was the whiteness in her that made her different. She will tell you that she chose the darkest man she could find to date (my father) because she was so light and hated her skin. She never, ever wanted anyone to think she was white.

If this had been a few months later, after my mother cut her beautiful, straight "good" hair into a punk-looking fade an inch longer than Grace Jones', that white boy in my class would've never said that. And, for the record, my mother is no Carol Channing, no J. Edgar Hoover, she could never get away with pretending to be Italian, not light enough to *pass* pass. But, at that moment, to that child, she did. I didn't.

This led to my short stint as a liar. I began telling kids at school I was adopted. The white boy could authenticate the fact my mother was white. I told them my father was black, but that I was neither, and therefore, I was adopted. I said that. I was *neither*.

I wanted to be exotic. Ashland was typically Southern: Rich in history starting back from our country's founding, a town made up of only black and white people who lived segregated throughout. There were a few "others": One Southeast Asian family, two Korean sisters adopted by a local white family, the kid with a "Jamaican" accent who was really from Guyana, and later, when more Hispanic immigrants were moving into rural southern towns, we actually started to diversify—there were, at least, two or three immigrant families. I was learning Spanish then. My Spanish name was Veronica. In that part of a young person's mind, you know, that part that knows she is telling a lie, but wants so badly for that lie to be true, to reveal some new, interesting, unique and unusual thing about her, make her stand out, be different, turn her into a superstar—and yet, who still wants that lie to be a lie because she loves her parents—in that mixed up part of my mind, I was a Latina. I was *Veronica*. If I had to be anything at all.

This lasted maybe a week. I stopped telling that story one day at my cousin's house. We were swinging on the playground set she had in her backyard. I told her the tale: my mother is white, my father is black, and I am neither, so I am adopted. The lie, so fluid, was like water dripping from my lips.

She never broke the stride of her swing. "No you're not," she said.

I slowed down to a stop and asked, "How do you know?" as if she had some insight that I didn't, as if there were some real question as to whether or not I was actually adopted and secretly a Latina.

She said, "Because you're not," a slight shrug, a kick of her feet and she swung back so her legs went straight in the air, her face toward the sky.

C. A Brief History of Rape, Not Rape, and Other Confusing Facts:

- About 1851: A slave named "Mollie" gives birth to a son named Botts who is later listed as "mulatto" on the 1910 census. Botts is my great grandfather three times removed. I tried to search for his mother, but only found documents that said: "1, 20, F, B" or some variation thereof. She was a slave; I was never going to find more. I could've pretended to search for his father. Instead, I entered "Slaveholder Morris" into my family tree and moved on.

- I am a product of rape.

- I am a product of slavery.

• 1963: A sixteen-year-old descendant of Botts Morris has a baby by a man from two counties over who is fifteen years her senior and married with children her age. How this man and child met, I do not know. How this man and child had sex, I can only speculate. My mother claims the man's family was part white, but I never met him and she said he only came around a few times. So little, in fact, that when I asked her for her father's name, she did not know it, only that it was "Walker" or "Warren" or "William." The sixteen-year-old, my grandmother, leaves her daughter to be raised by her sister. She runs away from home, the poor country life, to live a more exciting one in the city, party with Marvin Gaye, dance the night away at Studio 54, have two more children she would also leave for someone else to raise and almost never speak of the man who fathered her first-born child, at least not to her granddaughter.

• I am almost 30% white, which means my European relative is close—a great grandparent or great, great grandparent—yet I have no concrete relative to point to, no one I can name.

• 1993: The granddaughter of the former sixteen-year-old descendant of Botts Morris will have her breasts fondled by a man while at her grandmother's house. The former sixteen-year-old descendant of Botts Morris will tell that granddaughter it was her own fault she was molested; the girl was too grown and always in a man's face.

• And now, I wonder whether my grandmother meant to say that to me or if she was talking out loud to herself.

III. Asian, less than 2%[8]

A. Charted on my computer screen brightly before my eyes in desensitized, deadening plainness were my AncestryDNA results, an entire history of slavery, rape, oppression—love, family, pride—simplified into graph form. Digesting this information physically impacted me as if all of those years and people had bum-rushed my body at once instead of slowing contributing to my blood year after year. Centuries at my fingertips, yet the only surprise was the trace Asian genes. I am still working out what all of this means to me. I do know my middle school self would've clung to this information as a badge of otherness, what made me different than all the other black girls whose DNA was exactly like mine. I am undeniably American. This spark of difference gave me a fluttering heart, though, a sense that something powerful had happened to someone in the long line of those who created

---

[8] Most of this percentage is from the Caucasus region which includes Armenia, Azerbaijan, Georgia, Iran, Iraq, Syria, and Turkey.

me. I imagine an ancient, Asian ancestor crossing the desert to become an African warrior or sailing the Pacific to settle this country and wind herself into the genetic fabric of Native Americans. But that is not what happened.

B. Instead, she followed a downing sun west, the brilliant, blazing orb bowing behind the horizon. Seventy years captive, the march from Babylon mimicked the way there—just without the chains. Further across the world, across a continent, her drowned feet dragged through orange sand, her footsteps disappearing with the wind like those of her mother and father a generation ago. Her mother had sung of Zion with King Jeconiah on the road to Babylon. Such cruel punishment: to demand mirth in the face of oppression as you confront no return, forcing a song, happiness at the moment of its antithesis. But they sang to not forget. "For we were slaves; yet our God has not forsaken us in our bondage, but has extended mercy to us in the sight of the kings of Persia, to give us a reviving, to set up the house of our God, and to repair the desolations thereof, and to give us a wall in Judah and in Jerusalem."[9] To be led out of bondage, yet still not be free.

---

[9] Ezra 9:9

A Nameless Mound

My ancestors haunt a dirt road called Egypt. At the end of the road, my aunt's bones rest beneath a rise of earth. Her grave is unmarked, and it is my fault. A clearing in the woods, our family's boneyard is full of other, older, nameless mounds and dead, red leaves. We used to tiptoe through those woods, my aunt and I, my little hand inside her big one. We watched our steps—bad luck to walk on a grave, you know; means you're next. Broomsticks in hand, we swept away leaves, whispering to her brothers and sisters: Pick, Pug, Fred, Bee. She made me sing "Jesus Loves the Little Children," told me about her mama when the swept-away leaves revealed "Bertha Coleman." She let my hand go, I mushed my nose, inhaled the ghost of Jean Naté.

She's right there beside them now. Their plotted arrangement: Great-Grandma Bertha, Aunt Bee, then her—skeletons of matriarchs, a row of bones once covered by light-brown, mole-pocked faces, relaxed hair still growing inside silk-lined boxes, cigarette-puckered cheekbones—high and arched 'cause you know we got Indian in us. But you wouldn't know she was there unless you knew she was there; unless you were there on the day we laid her down, touched my arm while I sat next to the casket in the woods, heard a rose thump her pearl coffin; unless you were at the church and felt my shoulders heave behind the first pew, the pew reserved for daughters, for husbands, for grandchildren—she had none of those, only me, a great-niece of twenty-eight no one trusted to get it right. And everyone spoke over me. And I forgot to give her grave a name. Her grave in the boneyard inside the hollowed space in the woods at the end of Egypt Road, where some poor ancestor of ours decided to cut down some trees, dig a hole, and lay a body, then cut another tree, dig another hole, lay another body—cut, dig, lay, cut, dig, lay—'til Colemans wandered Egypt-land like Israelites. An army of ancestors—the Coleman clan, a dying breed—march through Egypt, searching for their names. In the middle of the clearing they all stop: here lies Elizabeth Anderson née Coleman, with nothing but a dead, red leaf stuck to her mound.

But before I buried her, before she died, before the death rattle, before the hospice, before the phone call to come home, when we first admitted her to long-term care that turned out to be so short, I lay beside her crumbling body on the thin, nursing home mattress and held her small hand inside my big one. Evening had come, but the sun wanted to stay. It pushed through the shades, white light not going to be stopped for nothing, flicking between cracked salmon blinds like through the trees on Egypt Road, and her skin took on the iridescent gray of fish. I lay next to her, slipped a pearl ring off her finger, and placed it on my pinky. I held her hand; put my head to her shoulder, and I remembered when my mom was a teen mom and my aunt kept me after school. Off the bus, down Egypt, her trailer was tight: fat little boy figurines holding out arms saying I LOVE YOU THIS MUCH, Garbage Pail Kids cards over paneled walls because my cousin gave them to her and she never said no, *pictures*—me, school photos of my cousins, me, family I didn't know, family I'd just seen, me, her dead mother asleep in a casket, me—plants snaking the half wall between the kitchen and living room, Mahalia Jackson's alto moan, and pork-n-beans with burnt hot dogs. She never forgot a thing. Holding her hand, head on shoulder, I cried because fuck cancer! Sunlight still fighting through the blinds, she would die in that nursing home. Sixty-five, only sixty-five. The family we had left was there: her sister Patty, my mother, my soon-to-be-husband, my brother, me, me, me.

She never forgot me.

She breathed in, but not out, and the sun finally touched her.

Cut, dig, lay. Cut, dig, lay. The woods so tight spent too much time watching my step. For seven years: mortgages, bills, children, excuse, school, bills, excuse, excuse, excuse. And even if I do—*when* I do—I still never ordered the goddamn tombstone.

How to Mourn

"Everything's far away. Everything's a copy of a copy of a copy."

—The movie, *Fight Club*

If you read my fiction, you will find a character named Grandma. In real life, she is dead. This is the story of her death. A story this writer, the main character—T—began drafting the moment she knew Grandma was not long for this earth. A story more like a performance—the sensation of watching yourself from outside your own body, when everything feels unreal, like living in a dream. Or, at least for me, for T, like living in a story.

This story begins with T walking nursing home corridors on her way to see her very recently deceased grandmother. Nauseated from a too-sweet Starbucks latte and chocolate cookie, T is sick with worry wondering if nausea means she has diabetes. She probably does. It is what killed Grandma, you know. Complications of eating like a poor person: McDonald's, Captain D's, Wendy's, Walmart's fried chicken and mac-n-cheese. T eats like a poor person who is no longer poor and thinks she's too good for fast food: Starbucks, Chipotle, delivered Chinese, wine, wine, wine. Just more expensive ways to die.

She chugs at the end of a grief train behind her mother, her mother's friend, her stepfather, and her little brother. T disconnects from the real world. Muffled click-clacking shoes on black-flecked white tile, voices hushed, drowned by the roar of insufficient air conditioning and surreality, this facility is a prop or a set, fiction. Real life for T feels like fiction, especially in difficult times. T had, in fact, began drafting this tale in her mind on her way from Maryland to Virginia. Her writing music—Sam Cook and The Allman Brothers—played on her Pandora app. She headed back home to the country, and the country gathered to meet her, trees racing past I-95 South. Alone in her truck, she remarked to herself about how beautiful the day was, how her grandmother's death was an example of nature's beauty—or some other trite lie. Later in the evening, guilty over her lack of grief, her too rational, academic frame of mind, she asked friends if there was something wrong with her, if this lack of empathy, driven by a palpable desire to write, meant she was selfish. It wasn't the appropriate response T decided, despite her friends' reassurances.

Shuffling through winding nursing home halls, T's nausea becomes acute, now directly related to the smell of old. Every "elderly-person-dying" story has a scene where the narrator is sick from the nursing home or hospital smell. It is a cliché. This writer knows it. And if this were fiction, T would find some clever, not so overused way of representing this reality. But it's a cliché for a reason. Real life is a cliché.

They arrive at Grandma's room. Behind a white curtain... *beyond the veil* (yes, this writer could not help herself) lay her grandmother, or the vessel that carried her grandmother, now stiff and empty, a snail's shell. T's uncle and his girlfriend are already there. For an inmate, Uncle is clearly very much free, and he taps his ankle bracelet when T enters the room with the rest of the grief train to indicate he must head back to confinement, his work-release over at three. Uncle was Grandma's favorite, so she waited for him to arrive before she died. T cannot help but be miffed at this, although she tries to tamp down her anger. It is just like her grandmother, impatient and calculating 'til the day, to die the moment T finally arrives in Virginia after a two-hour drive, yet before she reaches the nursing home, because Uncle, Grandma's favorite, had finally made it there, and he was all she needed to move on. Fuck the rest of us.

The smell in the small room is a finger prying T's mouth open, trying to shove its way down her throat. No one has opened a window, and death has made it hot and damp and stale in the room. With hardly any space to fit them all around the bed, T's mother, the recurring character you may recognize as "Ma," shimmies past Uncle and Girlfriend, and pulls the curtain back. T stands behind them, on the other side, as close to the hallway as she can be. Ma stands inside the curtain, her husband's arm around her shoulders. Blocked by drapery, T can only hear *sniff sniff*, see her mother's hand move to press a tissue to the inside of her eyes. T stares at her feet. She has not shed a tear.

Ma stands there less than a minute. "You want to see her?"

T has seen a dead body before. She saw a person die. Unlike her grandmother, her great-aunt, Grandma's sister, waited until T arrived to die. Great-Aunt also perished in a nursing home, and now it occurs to T how similar Great-Aunt and Grandma's deaths are. If this story were made up, T would use this fact as the basis for some contrived scene of parallelism too convenient to not be deliberate, a narrative construct. But coincidences like this are all too common in low-income, black families to be intended narrative devices.

Fiction never gets real life right, though. It's always the parts of real life written in fiction no one seems to believe. What does T consider reality? A childless great-aunt who was more grandmotherly than the formerly loose and slutty grandmother? A grandmother so selfish she intentionally leaves nothing for her family, takes it all along to the other side of the veil with her last and dying breath? A woman who allowed her granddaughter to be molested in her own home? So jealous, they physically fought? So jealous, Grandma told her the abuse was her fault? A woman who…T can go on for days, she knows the stories so well. The memories are too raw for her to feel real now. So vivid, indeed, that she wonders whether she made them up. Oh, if only she had.

In the back room of her grandmother's house, T learned how to escape. Watching *Reading Rainbow*, devouring *Sweet Valley High*, Choose Your Own Adventure stories, *The Babysitter's Club*, feet planted flat against the bedroom wall, T read books above her face, sometimes hanging her head off the edge of the full-sized bed she shared with her aunt. She read at night when the noise from the living room was too much to watch television. There was always a party going on. She wasn't allowed to leave the back room, but when she did—to go pee or to get a glass of Sprite—her eyes watered from the cigarette smoke. It hung solid in the air, blocks of gray cliffs floating through the small rooms. Even then, before she wrote, she imagined the smoke was a gas attempting to invade her body, choke her to death. And at night, when they were all gone, but the smoke lingered, it turned into a man, tall and dressed in black, coming to take her life away. He stood in the door crack or at the foot of her bed watching her sleep. She felt his presence, although there was no one. She learned to sleep lightly so she could always see if he was coming. Was he coming? No. He was already there.

Was always there—an amalgamation of those men who on those party nights danced in the living room with Grandma or her aunts or her cousins. Those men who drank and waited for her to leave the back room and come out front so they could grab her wrist with hard, dry hands grinding into the tender flesh of her forearm as she tried to wrench away; so they could laugh at the scared little girl interrupting the grown folk's party; so she could run to the back room, put her feet on the wall, open a book, press the scratchy paper to her face, harder, so she was almost inside it, harder, so if she pressed more, she would end up on the other side of it, harder, onto the inside where the story was now real life, and far, far away.

———————

If this were fiction, we would've gotten to this part by now. The part where T pulls back the curtain and sees her dead grandmother's body, sitting up in a Craftmatic-style hospital bed. Grandma's silver, thin hair stretches across her head, brown scalp peeking through the lines of white cotton. Her body is stiff, and her eyes are closed. But what T notices first, what T becomes irritated by, fixated on, what will haunt T in the middle of the night as she tries to sleep, is her grandmother's open mouth. An oval slimming her face downward. The Ghost screaming in the Munch painting. T knows it's where Grandma's soul escaped from. She crept out of her own mouth, the snail shell now rigid.

"Can they close her mouth," T says.

"They had her on oxygen," Ma responds.

"Well, why can't they close her mouth?" The heat of irrational anger replaces her nausea. Why would they leave her looking like that?

Ma sits hesitantly on the neat little bed of Grandma's missing roommate. "The funeral director can fix it."

T glances at her grandmother one last time before walking out of the cramped room and to the benches outside. In no way does Grandma resemble Great-Aunt in death. There is agony on her grandmother's face, the silent scream of a person taken before she wanted to go. And indeed, she had suffered more than Great-Aunt, who had cancer and was prepared, mentally and spiritually, to die. T had conversations with Great-Aunt, had been there to tell her she loved her, had held her hand, was given a pearl ring in remembrance. The hospice nurse was a Christian, T's former classmate. They prayed and prayed to themselves, filling the silent room with the noise of their thoughts, their own fear of dying suspended when confronted by the real thing.

Great-Aunt took a breath, then life fell limply out of her, a crumpled tissue dropping from an open hand.

T doesn't know what happened when her grandmother died. She wasn't there. She imagines it was less graceful. Grandma must have been pleading or trying to breathe, to take in as much air, oxygen, life as she could to make a mouth so broad and stiff. Later, T went home to her father's and tried to sleep, but when she closed her eyes all she could see was the black hole of her grandmother's gaping mouth, waiting to suck her in.

The exit at Lewistown Road off of Virginia I-95 used to be easier to navigate. Large Mack trucks barrel toward T in a turn-off lane wide enough to fit three of the monster-sized vehicles beside her in a row. If you take a left at the exit, you'll pass the truck stop. The large orange and blue "76" sign approaching her on the highway gives T tingles in her stomach on her way down for Grandmother's funeral.

She makes that left, goes to the stop sign, turns right onto Ashcake Road. Dead, golden grass, small houses with concrete rocks as gravel for driveways, homes made of cinderblocks with a semi parked out front line Ashcake. Egypt Road is on the right, but she almost passes by it. There used to be a dilapidated, white house at the start of the road. The white family who bought the land on Ashcake right next to Egypt claimed the particular spot was on their property and tore it down.

T has refused to drive down Egypt since Grandma made them lose the house T grew up in. Before Grandma had a stroke and was placed in the nursing home, Ma offered to arrange for

Habitat for Humanity to come in and remodel the house, or rather, tear it down and build a new one. T had given birth to twins, Ma's first grandchildren. Ma wanted there to be a home in the country where they could come and stay, know their family, play with their cousins. All Grandma had to do was add Ma to the deed. Ma would take care of it. Grandma didn't have to do a thing.

Grandma said no. It was her house. That was it.

It was this act of selfishness that stopped T from caring anymore, the reason T avoided visiting Grandma at the nursing home. Later, when Ma had to sell the house because Medicare would not allow Grandma to have any assets, Ma shared the bill of sale and the deed with T. Another great-aunt had "sold" the house to Grandma in the 80s for ten dollars.

So, on the day of Grandma's funeral, T is forced to drive by the house for the first time in a long time. The grass is a mile high. The house, a small rancher of no more than 500 square feet with four rooms and a bathroom, seems sunken, halfway hidden by the bush with only the upper half sticking out like the tip of a cat's head peeking through the grass before it pounces. T tries not to imagine herself inside there, especially in the back room where she slept, but the memories are as real as the grass, although as faint as the house hidden within it. She fights the familiar comfort of this place, especially the joy wanting to creep inside her, wanting to attack the anger she desperately will not let go.

Here, in this memory, her grandmother sits on the living room couch, sharing some gossip she's heard about a cousin. They are laughing. She hears her grandmother's laugh, and it isn't a cackle. No, too convenient. Her grandmother's laugh is sly, knowing, indulgent, a smile you know once dripped of cognac and music and heavy eyelids, of being fabulous and young and adored and all the things T had felt inside herself at one point or another. Worldly. Grandma's thoughts—smarter, wittier, faster than yours—always betrayed the smile and sound from her mouth through the slant and glisten in her eyes. Not sinister or nasty, despite the way it sounds, but admirable— the way a grown-ass woman ought to laugh, when you think about it.

T heard her grandmother laugh the most when her brothers and sisters were around and the late night parties included everyone on Egypt Road, or everyone in Brown Grove, the name this community of black folks calls itself. A whole generation is gone now with her grandma. All eleven Coleman children, Grandma and her siblings, each one raised on that plot of land with the sunken house, are dead, evidence of their existence hiding in the woods of Egypt Road: their bones beneath the ground. T might cry for the first time since her grandma passed at the thought of this. But, she doesn't.

T drives past Grandma's, down to her cousin's house situated next to the suspended wooden platform that used to be attached to her Great-Aunt's home. Great-Aunt lived in a trailer at the end of the road. Now only the porch remains. T does not want to be there. She sits in her car, only getting out to greet her family as they arrive, then returning to her safe space. She is afraid if she leaves this space, she will no longer be able to hold on to her anger. Anger is all that feels real to her. If she lets it go, the glass screen separating her emotions, tethering her to this third person narrative, will shatter and break. She is not ready to feel anything more, not yet.

She stares at the thin air that used to be Great-Aunt's home. It's better that the trailer is gone now instead of still standing like her grandmother's house.

They had to sell Grandma's house.

You know, she died the day before closing.

———

There were stories about her grandma, how she lived her young life before she came back to the county in her late thirties because of diabetes. T believed the stories, especially the ones Grandma told herself. Right after, Grandma lost her leg because of diabetic complications and bad circulation (like the rest of her brothers and sisters), but she was still thin and had her looks.

She drove her car, using one foot to pedal the gas and the break on her Shadow Gray, 1989 Nissan Datsun. Grandma was full of stories. Frankie Beverly from Caroline. You know he our cousin. We partied with Marvin Gaye. We danced all night at Studio 54. Ain't no one have nothing on me!

T learned the power of a woman from watching the women in her family, and even with one leg, Grandma dated men half her age. She always seemed to come alive around young people. She offered drinks to T and her college friends when they came to visit, gossiped with T when they were alone—somehow the sick-and-shut-in knew everyone's business. She dyed her hair honey blonde until it turned gray, jet black until it fell out, then continued to perm it perpetually straight. Kept herself up until she finally gave up, when her self-esteem and selfishness collided, and she could not bear to be seen in public, morbidly obese with only one leg.

She'd had her first child at sixteen by a married man twice her age. Left her children to be raised by her sisters or given up for adoption. Let that white man visit her during the day, alone, and when he left, took his money. Yet, in her death, she seemingly left us all with nothing—not even those stories (Frankie Beverly is from Philadelphia, not Caroline County, Virginia).

T sought the seduction that thread through her grandmother's stories. There were no Marvin Gayes or Frankie Beverlys, but spring break on South Beach, topless on the sand. Many boys, then later, many men, she used and let use her because sex was all each other was worth. Dancing and drinking herself into blackouts. Wandering the streets alone until she ended up in strange hotel rooms, waking the next day with only a headache and no remorse. A self-indulgent fantasy, T now the antagonist. Her childhood diary lost, she had no way to escape except to live her own fiction.

Cars and pick-up trucks crowd the church's parking lot where the funeral will take place. Black suits dart from the ground topped with freshly shaven brown faces. Braided crowns and Isoplus gelled weaves cluster in cigarette smoking hives near open car doors across the road. Sunglasses, sweating faces, laughter, do-gooding, hugs, all exposition to her story. Grandma is the main character today, whether you knew her or not, whether she was the same character for you as she was for everyone else, or not.

T considers Grandma's legacy while lined up in front of the church before the funeral. It is surprisingly packed. Behind her are Uncle's children. One of his daughters has a son who looks so much like Uncle, he could've spat the boy out.

"You wait," she says to her half-sisters, "see what happens when you have one."

"That's why I'm not having any kids," one of the others responds.

T's cousins, Uncle's kids, comment on how they never met Grandma, didn't know her. They know T's mother. One of her cousin's sounds as if she is about to say something smart or nasty about T's mom, but another cousin silences her sister because T is standing right there.

This is the real story Grandma has left behind. One of loss, evidenced by the fact T's first cousins don't even recognize who she is standing less than two feet away, and by the fact Uncle is also within earshot of his own children talking shit.

They march into the church and sit. T is at the end of the pew, glad to be alone. The pastor preaches about being right with God, and Grandma told him when he visited her in the hospital she wanted to be "right with God." His implication is she wasn't before. His sermon, in fact, implies a whole lot: Grandma was a sinner, she lived a fast life, and she had much to repent for. His voice rises and falls in the fake cadence of someone who imagines himself a great orator, but he is no Martin Luther King, no T.D. Jakes. He strains to pull emotion from the audience well before the eulogy even begins. Anger burns T's face, her shoulders, and arms. This is not his story to tell. The tale of Grandma's indiscretions belongs to T and her cousins, to Ma and her uncles. How can this so-called man of God, who says the Almighty is the final word, sit at the altar of our Lord and Savior and announce Grandma's sins to the world? T wishes she was sitting next to her mother right now. She would squeeze her mom's hand, stare her in the eye, trying to communicate her thoughts about this mess, then they would shake their heads in unison at the ridiculousness.

But, Grandma's three children are sitting in the first two rows far from T. Ma is in the front pew crying. Behind her sits Uncle, a man who has done hard time. He also cries. Next to him is Grandma's other son, the one she officially gave up for adoption. He cries, too. Grandma never raised him, in fact, she only raised Uncle, for the most part, yet all of her children weep. This unnerves T, surprises and shames her. Did she not have the story right? Yes, the pastor was wrong in putting Grandma's sins out there in the world, but still, even still, T knew the man's account of the woman wasn't too far off. In that case, what was there to cry about? Was there something about her grandma, about this character, she missed?

In the days before the funeral, when T and Ma were working out the issues caused by Grandma's unexpected passing, Ma mentioned she believed Grandma died the day before the house closed on purpose. T laughed, thinking her mother was referring to her grandmother's unwavering stinginess, and in a way, she was. "You know your grandma was always tight with a dollar," her mother's voice light, "that's why she died before anyone else could get her money. She made sure her children could keep it."

———

One of my favorite scenes in the movie *Fight Club* is when Edward Norton's character violates the fourth wall and speaks directly to the camera about all the ways Tyler Durden fantastically does not give a shit. Previously, the unnamed narrator recounts his life inside what the viewers imagine is his head. We hear a voice speaking, telling us what is happening on screen while the person who is talking acts out what the voice is saying. The other characters on screen behave as if they cannot hear this voice, which mimics how real life thoughts occur, and therefore, we as the viewer understands this to be the recounting of a story in someone's mind or, another possibility, to someone who is off camera. Just not directly to us. This is how the first person works in a film. When we read a story or essay, never do we consider the narrator is speaking to us. Nor do we recognize our participation in the telling of his story, because, even as we watch a story, or even as we read a story, we imagine it is being told to the character's unnamed friend, someone other than ourselves. To recognize the story is being told to you spoils your anonymity, the voyeurism involved in watching a movie inside a dark theater or enjoying a good read while in bed.

However, when Edward Norton turns directly to the camera, to those watching, and speaks, we are forced to acknowledge the performance of the previous narration. We are watching a show, and we are part of the show. No more hiding.

I find this quote from Seymour Chatman, a film and literary critic who studied narrative and narrative structure, illuminating to my personal ruminations on why I write. He said, "When I enter the fictional contract, I add another self: I become the implied reader." It bothered me, truly saddened me how I was more concerned about writing about my grandmother dying than I was about her actual death. When I sat to write the story, an unrealized grief over my lack of empathy drew me to the third person. So different from our self-aware narrator from *Fight Club*, yet he turned out to have multiple personalities. It is all so confusing, this being a writer and being a human being, and wishing your real life wasn't true sometimes. As Chatman suggests, though, it boils down to the audience and the fictional contract. If the naratee and the implied reader coalesce, if we are narrating our own stories, a story unique to our own lives, a story in which only we can know the real meaning, one in which we only know the past, present, and future, then, who are we writing for? Why does my own story sound better in the third person?

I thought this essay was about the question of why I write, primarily why I deflect emotions by writing instead of feeling them. Often times, it takes the ability to detach from a situation before I know how I feel about it, but in the course of considering whether or not I write because I want to feel, or because I want to forget, I've at least identified who my ideal reader is. She is black. She is educated. My reader is of any age, but whatever age, she is mature. She is not easily offended, nor is she a doormat. She understands my references; I don't have to explain myself. She reads not only for entertainment but for enlightenment, so she may go "huh" at the end of an essay and run her fingers through her natural hair and think, "ain't that some shit."

My cousin is called for a solo toward the end of the funeral service. Before she sings, she talks to the audience. Thirty years ago, on this same date, her father, Grandma's brother, was the first Coleman to die. This day, we honor the life of the last. We are family, she says. As she talks, my vision goes blurry. My face heats.

How long had I held on to anger? Like the white house at the beginning of Egypt Road, it gave me a map, a scion to my old life. Yet my grandmother was dead, and I was the only person angry. Yes, upset with her, but also mad at myself for acting as if I wasn't like her. I am self-absorbed, selfish, calculating, sly, writing this essay an act of selfish indulgence. I wanted to resemble my great-aunt, but I know I am a spitting image of my grandma. Is this essay for her then? Instead of an implied reader, instead of myself? Maybe she is the reason why I write.

During my cousin's solo, I stop ignoring the coffin a few feet in front of me. I never honestly acknowledged the nursing home scene as real. It was part of the essay, the story I began crafting the moment my mother called and said Grandma wasn't long for this earth. To me, Grandma was still lying in her nursing home bed, waiting for us all to come and visit her—even now it's hard not to imagine her there instead of nowhere I can see. I break through my own fourth wall. I stop seeing myself in the third person. And, I finally weep for my grandma.

Acknowledgments

Stories and essays from this collection have appeared in the following publications:

How To Sit in *PANK* magazine online

Why I Let Him Touch My Hair in *Brevity Magazine*

An alternative version of *Prom Night* in *The Stoneslide Corrective*

An alternative version of *I Am Karintha* in *The Doctor T.J. Eckleburg Review*

An alternative version of *Sacrifice* appeared in *storySouth*

An alternative version of *I Been Changed* in *Bayou Magazine*

V-Day in *Quaint Magazine*

Thoughts on My Ancestry.com DNA Results in *The Rumpus*

A Nameless Mound in *upstreet literary magazine* and was reprinted in *Redux: Work Worth a Second Run*

An alternative version of *How To Mourn* in the *Kenyon Review*.

Other Titles
from Mason Jar Press

I Am Not Famous Anymore
poetry by Erin Dorney

The Bong-Ripping Brides of Count Drogado
fiction by Dave K

Not Without Our Laughter
poetry by Black Ladies Brunch Collective

Notes From My Phone
memoir by Michelle Junot

Caligula's Playhouse
poetry by Stephen Zerance

Nihilist Kitsch
poetry by Matthew Falk

Learn more at masonjarpress.xyz